For Alfred – M.L.
For Oliver – S.H.

First published in Great Britain 2021 by Red Shed, part of Farshore
An imprint of HarperCollins*Publishers*
1 London Bridge Street, London SE1 9GF
www.farshore.co.uk

HarperCollins*Publishers*
1st Floor, Watermarque Building, Ringsend Road
Dublin 4, Ireland

Text copyright © Matt Lucas 2021
Illustrations of Matt Lucas copyright © Matt Lucas 2020, 2021
Illustrated by Sarah Horne
All other illustrations copyright © Sarah Horne 2020, 2021
Matt Lucas and Sarah Horne have asserted their moral rights.
With special thanks to Rebecca Lewis-Oakes

ISBN 978 0 7555 0258 5
Printed and bound by CPI Group (UK) Ltd, Croydon CR0 4YY
1

My Very Very Very Very Very Very Very SILLY BOOK of PRANKS

MATT LUCAS

ILLUSTRATED BY SARAH HORNE

RED SHED

hello how are you? actually dont answer because i cant hear you anyway here is another very very very very very very very silly book and this one is full of pranks you can do on people and also has stories of pranks that people have done throughout history but dont worry its not like a history lesson at school where you get told off because you didnt do your homework because you forgot because you were watching SpongeBob all night anyway i do hope you like this book and if you dont maybe you can give it to someone else but dont forget to glue the pages together first ha ha

PRANKSTER'S CHARTER

1. I will use my pranks to make people laugh, including the person I play the prank on.
2. I will never put myself or anyone else in danger.
3. I will never prank someone who doesn't like pranks.
4. I will always apologise if a prank goes wrong.
5. I will share my pranking knowledge with other pranksters to pass on the joy of pranking.

I, the Prankster, do solemnly swear that I will abide by the Prankster's Charter at all times.

Hello, These Are the Contents

PRANKS TO PLAY AT HOME

here are some pranks you can play on people that you live with but obviously if you do play pranks on people you live with (or anyone in fact) you must remember two things – firstly the prank must be funny for the person you play it on not just you and secondly if you are going to play a prank on someone you have to be prepared for them to play one on you too you cant just put a plastic rat in someones bed and then get all in a mood if they leave a rubber spider in yours . . .

. . . EW spiders EW NO THANK YOU
. . . even rubber spiders . . .
. . . EWWWWW

9

BROWNIE SURPRISE

Do you love cakes? Fake this bake to freak your family out!

Spend some time alone in the kitchen, banging pots and pans around and whatnot. Then call out, 'Who wants brownies?'

Everyone will come running, since they've heard you cooking up a storm. You wait in the kitchen holding a baking tin covered in foil. Use oven gloves to make it look realistic. Then pull off the foil and show the brownies . . . which are **ACTUALLY** capital letter 'E's cut out of brown paper! **Brown Es** . . . get it?!

Extra Prank Points: *with the help of a grown-up, make a* **real** *batch of brownies and bring them out after you've given everybody a good giggle.*

YUM!

i hope you can bake better than me i once made a cake but didnt read the recipe properly and didnt put flour in it and also eggs and sugar and baking powder and when it came out of the oven it was invisible

I JUST WOKE UP LIKE THIS

SHHHHH! Practise moving verrrrryyy quietly for this one.

Get up early (I know, I know, but it's worth it). Sneak **SILENTLY** into someone's bedroom and place a funny mask on the pillow next to them. When they wake up – **AAARRRGHH!**

12

BUG IN THE LIGHT

Put a toy bug - the **creepier** the better, an icky beetle maybe - on the inside of someone's bedside lamp. Then, when it's dark and they turn the light on, a **TERRIFYING** shadow will appear!

BUG UNDER THE MUG

Turn a mug upside-down and put it on the floor or table as if you've just trapped a spider or bug underneath. Put a note on the mug that says: 'Danger! Don't move this mug!'

Will anyone dare lift the mug? Sit back and laugh at their confusion if they do!

i never get scared and i know ghosts dont really exist and the only reason i still sleep with the light on is because i cannot find the light switch honest

BRRRRRRR -EAKFAST BOWL

Start this prank the night before.

Pour your little sister's favourite cereal into her bowl with some milk. Don't forget her spoon! Then ... put it in the freezer.

Now here's the hard part: **WAKE UP EARLY**. Put her frozen bowl on the table. She'll be all like, **'Ooh, thanks for making my breakfast!'**

WOW THANKS!

HEY!

the only thing is i am not good at waking up early in fact if it was up to me i would stay in bed all day but i would still go to school but my bed would be on wheels and i would do lessons in my pyjamas

THEN ... she won't be able to lift her spoon out of the frozen cereal! Ha ha ha ha ha ha HA!

Extra Prank Points: *make her some tasty toast and then throw it up in the air while you say* **'Let's raise a toast!'**

NO USE CRYING OVER SPILT MILK

You will need white glue, baking paper, an empty milk carton or bottle and ... patience!

Put a large piece of baking paper on a table. **CAREFULLY** pour glue into a funny 'spilt milk' shape. Wait for it to dry. **YAWN**.

Woohoo, it's dry! Now, place your empty milk carton or bottle on its side on the table. Peel the dried glue 'milk puddle' off the baking paper and put it next to the milk carton.

if you cannot find a milk carton in your fridge then make sure you work really hard in school and pass all your exams and then get a really good job and then you can buy one

Now . . . wait for your family to try and clean it up!

MILK

Extra Prank Points: make sure you're the first one into the kitchen, act shocked about the spilt milk and offer to clean it up yourself. **THEN** act surprised when it's not really wet. You'll deserve an Oscar if you can stop yourself from **sniggering!**

What's more annoying than being pranked when you're trying to get out of the house on time? NOTHING! Here are some hilarious ideas . . .

HALF A PAIR

Go to the shoe rack or cupboard and take one shoe from each pair. Hide the shoes around the house. Hide some right and some left shoes – see if anyone leaves the house in a non-matching pair
– **HA HA!**

STITCHED UP!

Stop your grown-up from putting on their jumper by loosely sewing up the cuffs and neck the night before. Ask another adult or older sibling to help - it'll be worth it!

BIGFOOT

Stuff tissue paper or newspaper in the ends of everyone's shoes to make them think their feet have grown.

also if you are very rich you can give someone a pair of slippers for christmas and also secretly buy an identical pair in a larger size and then switch them round and the person will think their feet have shrunk ha ha

KOOKY COOKIES

This one's super sneaky!

If there's leftover mashed potato (unlikely – mash is **SOOO** tasty), mix it with some black beans from a tin (you know, the ones that are already cooked). Then dollop it onto a baking tray to look like cookies. You could bake it in the oven, or not bother.

Proudly produce your delicious cookies on a plate. Everyone will think they're chocolate chip! (Don't forget to eat the 'cookies' afterwards. Don't let delicious mashed potato go to waste!)

Extra Prank Points: *mashed potato makes great fake 'ice cream' too!*

MAGICIAN'S KEYHOLE

You know that magician's trick where they pull a hanky out of their pocket but then it just keeps on coming? Well, it turns out it works with keyholes too!

Poke a long, thin ribbon through the front door keyhole (this only works with some kinds of lock) or the keyhole on a cupboard. Leave a tiny bit dangling down on the inside - the rest will be outside. In the morning, your grown-up will go to unlock the door, start to pull the ribbon out . . . then just keep pulling and pulling!

(Make sure you ONLY use ribbon - you do NOT want to get anything stuck in the lock.)

i like magicians but it annoys me when they dont tell me how they do their tricks and i nag them and nag them but then when they do tell me i just think oh

PRANK BUTTON

Use your crafting skills to make a large red button and stick it to a desk or table using BluTack. Add a note that says 'Don't press this button!'. Hide somewhere you can see the button and when someone presses it, deflate a whoopee cushion, fire up a fart machine or blow a horn . . .

SCHOOL RUN

Pick a Saturday or Sunday morning to get dressed for school. Get your school bag ready and everything. Now wake your grown-up in a panic, pretending that you're late. They'll be so relieved when they realise it's just a prank!

WATCH YOUR STEP

Heard of that gameshow *Floor is Lava*?
Go ahead and recreate it in your house.
NOT WITH ACTUAL LAVA, SILLY!

All you need are some (OK, a lot of) paper cups.
Fill the cups with something solid that won't
make tooooo much mess, for example, a small
toy, buttons or beads – or that weird white stuff
that comes in parcels that's a bit like Wotsits.
You could use water if an adult agrees.

Cover the entire floor with cups, from door to
window. Bonus points if you do it in super neat
straight lines. Make sure you can leave the room
and then wait for the prankee to open the door
... **ENJOY!**

*(Do not play this prank if you have little siblings
who like to put small objects in their mouths!)*

24

WARNING!!!!
DON'T TRY THIS
AT HOME!

YOU'LL GET IN
SOOOOOOOOOOO
MUCH TROUBLE!!

the next week turn their clothes upside down. Make this go on for as long as possible! Until they decide to get you back!

But if they DO get you back, you've got an **EVEN BETTER PRANK** coming . . .

Take all their clothes out of their wardrobe and drawers and hide them. Yes.

You could replace the clothing with something else silly, like loo rolls or toys, or just leave a note. Something like, 'You went out of style, your clothes have moved on'.

And finally . . . The pièce de resistance. The pièce de la prank. The most daring and devious prank of all . . .

if you are reading this book in australia then you will need to do this prank the right way up

ROOM UPSIDE DOWN

While someone is out, why not rearrange their room so everything is UPSIDE DOWN?

Hang their rug from the curtain rail, nail their desk chair to the ceiling ... Hang on, you'll definitely need a professional to help with this ...

BUT you could turn small things upside down – like all the books in their bookcase, so they have to read the spines the wrong way up. Or turn all their toys over. You could flip the alarm clock, over turn their laundry basket. You get the idea ...

You could really, REALLY annoy someone by doing this bit by bit so that they don't notice at first. Start with one book, then do a whole shelf. Then turn their posters upside down, then

MOVE THE WHOLE ROOM!

That's right. While your prankee is sleeping, sneak into their room and relocate EVERYTHING to a different room. Carefully place the bedside table and lamp - don't forget their teddy - in the exact same space as it was in their room. Then - and you'll need an older sibling or grown-up for this - MOVE THE SLEEPING PERSON and place them in their new 'bed'. When they wake up, they'll turn off their alarm clock and . . .

FREAK OUT!!!

also you could buy another house in another country and move them to there that would be funny too ha ha

EEEK! IT'S A MOUSE!

Put (removable) tape
over the bottom of
a computer mouse, where
its movement sensor is located.
Your adult won't understand why they can't
move the pointer on the screen!

Extra Prank Points: *instead of the
tape, stick a Post-it note to
the bottom of the mouse
with the message* **'HA HA
HA'** *written on it. OR dress
the mouse up like a real mouse . . .*

Extra Extra Prank Points:
*the prank above also works well
for the TV remote! Ha ha ha!*

PORTRAIT PRANK

Tell your friend you'd like to sketch them. Flip to a fresh page and make it look like you're doing a super detailed drawing. Stare at your friend as if you're trying really, really hard to get their nose and eyes and mouth just right. Say things like, **'Keep still'** and **'I don't think I've got your eyebrows quite right.'** Take **AGES** doing all this!

Finally pretend to be pleased with what you've done. Put your pen down and turn your pad round to show your friend. **TA-DA!** On the pad is . . . a smiley face!

PRANKS TO PLAY WHEN YOU'RE OUT AND ABOUT

one of the good things about playing
pranks when you are out and about is
that people are less likely to know who
you are so you can pretend to be someone
completely different and nobody will
know for instance next time you are in
a shop why not talk in a different accent
from your normal one and see if you can
get away with it ha ha although obviously
this might not work if the shopkeeper
already knows you because then they will
just think you are being a bit odd

31

CAR-HA-HA

What happens on a loooong car journey after you've played I Spy for the millionth time? Annoy the other passengers, that's what!

1. Ruin a Knock, Knock joke by answering, 'Come in!'

2. Hold your hand just in front of the face of the person sitting next to you. When they tell on you, say, 'Not touching, can't get mad. Not touching, can't get mad!'

3. When you have just left the house and you're at the very beginning of a long journey, say to the driver, 'Just drop me here, I can walk the rest.'

the problem with long journeys is i always need the loo so when i am older i am going to have a toilet built in the back seat of the car so we dont have to stop i apologise in advance for the smell

4. Ask your sibling to say 'toy boat' again and again as fast as they can. (It's basically impossible.)

5. Tell your sibling to answer the following questions: 'What's 1+1? What's 2+2? What's 4+4? What's 8+8?' Then ask them to name a vegetable. (They will almost definitely say carrot. It's SO weird!)

6. Ask them to say 'shop' ten times, then ask them, 'What do you do when you come to a green light?' They'll probably say 'stop'. You've tricked them . . . the answer is **'GO!'**

Sometimes you're not in the car. Sometimes you're walking. Don't worry! There are still plenty of pranks to be performed.

FREE MONEY

Stick a coin to the ground then hide nearby and watch as passers-by try in vain to pick it up. You'll need to use very sticky superglue for this one - so ask your grown-up to help! (And don't forget to remove the coin later.)

EXCUSE ME

Walk beside your friend, then reach round and tap them on the opposite shoulder. They'll look over and be confused when there's no one on the other side of them.

Repeat. Repeat. Repeat.

once i did actually find a pound coin in the street and i was so happy and i picked it up but it was dirty so i went to a shop and spent the pound on soap the whole thing was a bit rubbish to be honest

REVERSE LAMPPOST

OK, so sometimes you're with someone who doesn't like to be pranked. All is not lost. You can still make use of ordinary pavement furniture (yes, it's actually called that) for a fun prank.

Simply pretend to walk into the lamppost YOURSELF. **Sounds painful?** It isn't!

You can make this prank as elaborate as you like. Why not smear a spot of red lipstick on your hand before you leave the house, then as you pretend to bash into the lamppost, lift your hand up to cover your nose and secretly smudge the lippie on your face . . .

When you pull your hand away, it'll give everyone a shock! Make sure to say, **'OW, OW, MY NOSE!'** as well.

Or why not go **ALL OUT** . . .

Get the face paints out and draw some very dramatic pretend injuries. Ketchup or jam looks great as fake blood. Create a fake arm out of papier mâché (see opposite), hide your other arm inside your sleeve and wave the fake one around until it falls off? You could even paint yourself grey or green using face paints and convince your family you've been bitten by a monster! Yeah, totally realistic.

Making papier mâché

You'll need newspaper, flour, water and a mixing bowl. Tear the newpaper into strips. Next mix flour and water into a runny paste in a mixing bowl. Dunk the strips of newspaper till they're nice and soggy. To make a fake arm, scrunch dry newspaper into an arm shape (you could wrap clingfilm around the 'arm' to help it stay in shape. Now cover the arm with the wet newspaper strips and leave them to dry. Add several layers, letting each one dry before adding the next. Once your 'arm' is completely dry, paint it skin colour.

Ta-da!

PHONE PRANKS

There's always one grown-up messing about on their phone at the table instead of paying attention politely at a restaurant, isn't there? Teach them a lesson! (If you don't have a phone, ask a helpful adult or friend to lend you theirs.)

SETTING THE TONE

Next time you're out for a family meal, get a bored uncle or mischievous grandma to help you. Secretly take your parent's phone and change the ringtone. Make it **SUPER ANNOYING.**

SMASH!

Ask a willing adult prankster to help you download a cracked screen app. Oops! Or take a picture of you with your face smushed-up against a window. Make it the prankee's screensaver so it looks like you're trapped inside the phone!

CHATTERBOX

Some people still TALK on the phone instead of texting. I know, like they live in the Dark Ages or something. Here are some ways to prank them into the twenty-first century! Sit next to someone who's on the phone and:

- loudly take part in the conversation, as if the person at the other end was talking to you
- loudly take part in the conversation, but pretend to be on YOUR phone – as if you're having the exact same conversation!

its so annoying whenever i buy a mobile phone there is a new one released a few months later so ive decided im just going to wait till they make the very last phone ever and then buy that

FACE FACTS

Here's one to trick a vain friend. Say, **'Oh my goodness, you look totally stunning today. Can I take a picture?'** Whip out your phone and pretend to take a snap.

Before doing that, prepare a photo of a sneezing camel (or llama - any **large, hairy animal** will do). Show your friend the picture - as if it's the one you've taken of THEM!

PESKY PINGS

In a crowded place, make your phone play a **'ping'** notification sound. Watch while everyone reaches for their phone and is disappointed when it's not them who's got a new message. Very, very simple . . . very, very infuriating!

ALL DRESSED UP

Do you belong to a sports club or team? Here's a fun way to prank your teammates!

Turn up to sports practice wearing the wrong kit. Going swimming? Wear your football kit – and act like nothing's wrong. Ha ha!

Does one of your teammates love pranks? Make them laugh by getting all of the REST of the team to get dressed for a different sport. They'll be so confused, they'll think it's THEM who's got it wrong . . . until they catch on and find your prank HILARIOUS!

PRANK PROJECT

This is an old, old trick. It's still magnificent.

This prank works well if you have a tall wall or bush in front of your house, or live on a safe street corner. Be measuring something and acting like you're really concentrating. Lots of 'HMMMM', and holding up a ruler or set square or anything fancier you can find at home.

THEN FIND AN UNSUSPECTING FAMILY MEMBER. Tell them you need their help with a school science project. Say you're trying to get accurate measurements of your home environment. Hand them the end of a ball of string and say, 'Please could you hold this just for a minute?'

Walk backwards away from them, unrolling the string. Then . . . **DISAPPEAR** round the corner out of sight.

Wait to see how long they hold it for.
HA HA HA!

Extra Prank Points: get **TWO** people to hold the mystery piece of string – one at each end.

if you cannot find a piece of string you could use a stick of celery i suppose but it would have to be a very very long one

TRICKY TRIANGLE

Turn to page 153 for a sneaky word prank to play on your friends next time you're out and about...

Show the image to your friends and tell them to read the words as fast as they can. Did any of them spot the mistake? Have YOU spotted it yet?

THE BIGGEST PRANKS IN HISTORY

i wish they would actually teach stuff like
this in history lessons at school it would
be much more better rather than going
on about christopher columbus discovering
america all the time like so what he didnt
build it he just found it it was already there
i found a ladybird on my arm will they
be telling future generations
about that i dont think
so somehow

TA
-DA!

45

THE COTTINGLEY FAIRIES

Do you believe in fairies? These fairy photos fooled the whole world for nearly 70 years!

The year is 1917. Elsie Wright, 16, and her cousin, Frances Griffiths, 9, kept being told off by their parents for coming home muddy. Like girls weren't supposed to play outdoors! Hmph, they thought, we'll show them . . .

'We've been playing by the stream with **fairies**!' said the girls, and they borrowed Elsie's dad's camera to prove it. Their photos looked **SO** realistic that their parents believed them, and so did lots of other people, including Arthur Conan Doyle, the super-famous author of *Sherlock Holmes*!

Now, I know what you're thinking. Errr, I can draw fairies onto photos on my phone

i took an amazing photo once but the gallery owner made me put it back

any time. **BUT - NO!** Back in the Olden Days, you had to take photos with an actual camera. And there were no computers or filters or those funny apps that jazz up your pics. Photos were photos, end of.

Arthur Conan Doyle asked an expert to examine the fairy photos, and he confirmed that they had been not been faked. Conan Doyle gave the girls a new camera and more photographic plates (which is what went into cameras before film). They took more fairy photos and the experts checked them again: the girls had not drawn on the plates.

47

Arthur Conan Doyle was delighted. The girls' photos **proved** that fairies existed! Yay! He published the story in a newspaper and **LOADS** of people believed it.

It wasn't until 1983 that the hoax was revealed. Elsie and Frances admitted they had faked the photos using cut-outs of fairies, held up with long hatpins so it looked like they were floating.

Hat(pin)s off to Elsie and Frances. They kept their secret nearly their whole lives. That's a long time to prank the entire world!

if fairies did exist i would ask one to fly up to the top of the kitchen cupboard and get me down that Pot Noodle because even on tiptoe i cant reach it

UNICORN, TRUE-NICORN

**Don't believe in fairies? How about ...
UNICORNS?!**

When an online shop started advertising 'canned
unicorn meat', customers loved the joke. So the
store started selling it – as a toy unicorn in a can.
How silly is that? Not silly enough for German
customs officials. They refused to allow the
(pretend!) cans of 'unicorn meat' into the country.
'Rare animal meat' is banned in Germany!

In 2012, the British Library in London made
an amazing discovery: a long-lost medieval
cookbook with a recipe for roasted unicorn!
'Taketh one unicorne,' it began, then marinade
it in cloves and garlic ... The 'author' of the book
was Geoffrey Fule. Fule ... Fool ... COME ON,
YOU'D GUESS THAT WAS FAKE, RIGHT?!

SPAGHETTI TREES

This pasta prank cooked up by the BBC in 1957 is one of the best hoaxes of ALL TIME!

Now, if you didn't know, spaghetti is made from wheat, semolina and water. Not according to BBC news programme *Panorama* though. They travelled all the way to Switzerland to film the annual spaghetti tree harvest.

The report showed farmers gathering spaghetti strands from the trees and explained how the mild winter had been perfect for a good spaghetti harvest. Yum! Of course, the farmers were actors and the report was a hoax!

Some people like to eat spaghetti with meatballs but i prefer a knife and fork

BEARSKIN

Would you believe that the fur on the bearskin hats the Queen's guardsmen wear actually KEEPS GROWING?

In April 1980, the official British Army magazine, *Soldier*, featured a story about how the fur that comes from Russian bearskin is is so thick, it keeps growing even when it's on a helmet and not a bear! They even showed photos of soldiers in an army barber shop having their helmets trimmed.

OF COURSE IT'S NOT TRUE. Can you imagine if the fur kept growing while the soldiers were on parade? They'd all bump into each other – **BONK!**

ANTARCTIC TREE PRANK

Sometimes people go a VERY long way to pull off the perfect prank...

A group of scientists were on an expedition in the Antarctic. Now, I know you're a geography genius, so I know you know that the Antarctic is where the South Pole is and it is VERY cold, VERY remote, and not much grows there. Only penguins. There are also lots of mountains and going anywhere is really tough. Still, some people like to try and hike there. **Weird.**

Anyway, these scientists were hiking up a steep icy cliff face in the Antarctic. It was really hard and they were really tired and – lo and behold – they beheld a TREE at the top of the next cliff. They could not believe their eyes.

WARNING! BY NOW YOU SHOULD KNOW THAT THIS MEANS YOU REALLY SHOULD NOT BELIEVE YOUR EYES.

The scientists thought, Whoa, we will be the super scientists who discover the first tree in the Antarctic! Everyone will think we are so clever and tough and amazing. So they started a long, hard and dangerous hike up to the tree.

They got there. They looked at the tree. It was **very** bright and **very** green. It was **a plastic tree.** They'd wasted all that time!

But just think . . . what top prankster put the fake tree there in the first place?!

what a TREE-MENDOUS prank ha ha sorry this is the worst joke i ever made

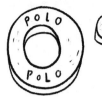

FREAKY FOOD

Can you tell food FACT from food FICTION?
(Clue: it's ALL fiction! This is a PRANKS book!)

MINTY MADNESS

In 1995, Polo Mints fans panicked when they
were told that foods with holes were about to
become illegal! **NO MORE HOLES!** The company
even joked that existing Polo Mints would
get with a set of 'hole fillers' to stay
within the law!

TELLING WHOPPERS

Burger King wanted to join the fun and in 1998
they advertised a new 'Left-Handed Whopper',
with all the same ingredients but flipped on
the bun so it would be better balanced for
left-handed eaters. What?!? When did they
launch this tasty treat? 1 April, of course . . .

MUSICAL VEG

Ever heard of a whistling carrot?
In 2002, the supermarket Tesco
said they had grown a special type of
carrot with holes in. When cooked, you
could blow in the top, and the carrot
would whistle . . . as loud as a pneumatic drill!
Really?! No. But tons of grown-ups believed it
and complained!

MOO-VE ON!

A hybrid is when two things are combined to
make a single thing. Like, a zedonk is a cross
between a zebra and a donkey (yes, really!).
So when scientists said they'd crossed a COW
and TOMATO to make a hybrid called a 'boimate',
lots of people were excited. Sillier yet, the fake
researchers were called MacDonald and Wimpey,
from the University of Hamburg. For real?!

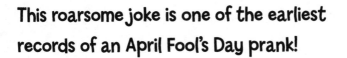

LIONS IN A LATHER

This roarsome joke is one of the earliest records of an April Fool's Day prank!

In the Olden Days, kings and queens loved to collect exotic animals, and often sent them to each other as gifts. The Tower of London was home to leopards, elephants, lions and even a polar bear, which was trained to catch fish in the River Thames.

On 1 April 1698, a cheeky prankster invited Londoners to come to the Tower to witness **'The Washing of the Lions'** ceremony in the moat. People came flocking. But it was all a hoax! They really should have guessed . . . because everyone knows lions like a nice warm bubble bath, not a chilly moat!

ELEPH-ANTICS

It's amazing what you can do with some ordinary white paint . . . and an elephant!

Over one thousand paying customers came to Frankfurt Zoo on 1 April 1949 to see a legendary snow-white elephant. Newspaper ads said it had come all the way from Burma and would be at the zoo for just one day. **AND THERE IT WAS!** An actual snow-white elephant.

Except . . . it was really an ordinary grey elephant PAINTED WHITE. The crowd was duped! Would you be cross if you'd paid a whole Mark (Germany's money back then) to see a fake white elephant? I would. BUT NO ONE MINDED! The zoo's director confessed it was all his idea. He was just trying to keep the zoo in business after the chaos of World War II. Good prank!

LEONARDO DA PRANKSKI

Have you heard of Leonardo da Vinci, the guy who painted the very famous, very old famous painting, the Mona Lisa? Well, he was also an incredible inventor! He drew designs for the first helicopter, as well as inventing early solar power, the parachute and loads of - yawn - geometry.

Well, Leo was sooo clever and so worried someone would find his amazing inventions and take all the credit that he wrote in his notebooks BACKWARDS. That's right, he wrote right to left, so you could only read his notes in the mirror.

TRY PUTTING A MIRROR UP AGAINST THIS PAGE TO SEE WHAT HE DID!

ooh thats better i was all dizzy there for a minute

Some people say the backwards writing was a way for Leonardo da Vinci to hide his genius ideas, but others say it was because he was left-handed and writing from right to left stopped him from smudging the ink as he wrote.

Whatever the reason, Leonardo totally pranked people trying to sneak a look at his notebook. **Bravo, Leo!**

SALON OF FAKES

Welcome to the Salon of Fakes! A marvellous museum of mostly made-up exhibits . . .

Kouros Statue

The Getty Museum in the USA paid SEVEN MILLION pounds for this Ancient Greek statue. It was so perfect, it looked too good to be true. **IT WAS TOO GOOD TO BE TRUE!** But weirdly, the museum still kept the fake on display. What would YOU buy with seven million pounds?!

Fake Vermeer

Way back in the twentieth century, an artist called Han van Meegeren made fake versions of famous

paintings, using clever tricks to make them look super old. His fake Vermeers sold for millions but . . . he was caught and went to jail. D'oh! Maybe don't try this one at home!

Tiara of Saitaphernes

This weird hat is actually a golden crown and it's 5,000 years old. (That's older than the Romans!) At least, this is what everyone THOUGHT. It turned out to be a fake. The goldsmith who made it almost got away with it, but his friend saw him at work . . . and spilled the beans!

Silly Salon

Yes, there really was an exhibition of fakes, and it included EIGHT forgeries of the *Mona Lisa*! Everyone really loves that painting!

TAKING A LEAP

In 1976, a very serious astronomer convinced a lot of people to do a very silly thing . . .

He told them that if they jumped in the air at exactly 9:47 a.m., they would float. Yes, **FLOAT!** He explained it was because, at that exact moment, the planets would all align and gravity on Earth would be weaker than usual. He even gave it a fancy scientific name: the Jovian-Plutonian Gravitational Effect.

OF COURSE, it was 9:47 a.m. on 1 April, so it was just a GREAT BIG COSMIC JOKE! Still, loads of people fell for it – or should I say, jumped for it.

HA HA!

LUNGS AWAy!

Flying without an engine? YOU wouldn't be fooled by this one, would you?

In 1934, newspapers all around the world printed a photograph of German pilot Erich Kocher and his amazing lung-powered flying machine. That's right, I said LUNG-powered. Erich was flying using his **BREATH!**

No one noticed that the name Kocher was originally spelled 'Koycher' – a German pun on 'keuchen' which means to puff or wheeze. AND MORE IMPORTANTLY, you can guess what day the photo was first published, can't you . . .

That's right. **1 APRIL!**

ROOFTOP CAR

The greatest student prank of all time!

One morning in 1958, the citizens of Cambridge woke up to find a **CAR** on a rooftop in the city centre. A car! On a rooftop! **HOW DID IT GET THERE?!** There were no security cameras back then, and everyone was mystified.

It remained a mystery for over 50 years. Finally, some former university students claimed the prank. They had removed the car's engine,

there isnt a car on the roof of my house i dont think but there is a chicken nugget which my mate threw up there for a laugh but then a cat ate it anyway

before hitching it onto ropes and swinging it onto the roof, all in the dead of night. They hadn't said a word for fear of being expelled!

SMELL-O-VISION

While telly was still pretty new, there was another famous BBC prank.

It was 1965 and the BBC reported that scientists had worked out how to transmit smell through the TV. Viewers watched as a 'professor' demonstrated his invention using coffee beans. Some were actually fooled into thinking they could smell coffee wafting from their TV sets!

This prank goes under the banner of 'just believable enough'. If you have someone who sounds like an expert, you can encourage people to believe anything. Like, next time someone insists you eat broccoli, you can say, 'Ah, but Professor Green from the Expert Institute of Genius says it's actually bad for children . . . you can't argue with science.'

i like the idea of this because you could do a blow-off when Emmerdale is on and then just say it was one of the cows

FAKE NEWS

Every year silly grown-ups fall for April Fools by Google . . .

As we've seen, it's amazing what grown-ups will believe. One year, Google pretended to launch a service called **Gmail Paper**, which was emails . . . but printed on (recycled) paper. Sort of defeats the point of emails, right?! But grown-ups ACTUALLY BELIEVED IT!

Other Google pranks included:

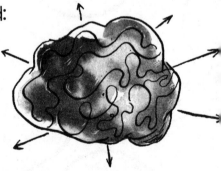

★ **Google Wind** – a machine that can blow away the clouds.

★ **Gmail Motion** – opens emails, replies or forwards them with just a wave of your hand.

> if you are not sure what Google is just google it

★ **MentalPlex** – who has time to TYPE a Google search? MentalPlex reads your mind and puts your thoughts straight into the computer!

★ **Google Scratch and Sniff** – place your nose next to the monitor and sniff. Oh, come on!

★ **Google Animal Translator** – 'Bridging the gap between animals and humans', or so Google claimed. **Ridiculous, right?**

AWESOME ANIMALS

Some of these animal pranks are SO OBVIOUSLY UNTRUE you'd have to be completely BONKERS to believe them! I guess the grown-ups who fell for them forgot that they ALL appeared on 1 April. Can YOU spot what's a FOOL and what's a FACT?

PENGUIN PRANKSTERS

In 2008, the BBC made the first EVER film of flying penguins, migrating from their home in icy Antarctica to the warm South American rainforest for winter. **FOOL!** Penguins can't fly! But so many people believed it, the BBC released a video showing how they created the special images!

PHONEY PONIES

In 1961, an Italian newspaper reported a new law
that all horses (still ridden for transport by many
people) had to be fitted with signals and brake
lights, just like cars. Even though this was a **FOOL**,
many people took their horses to car mechanics!
That one makes **NEIGH** sense!

SEEING DOUBLE

In 1996, scientists told the world about
a completely crazy experiment. They had taken
one sheep and made an identical copy, the same
in every way. The sheep was called Dolly and the
clever science thing was called 'cloning'. Can you
imagine TWO versions of you, exactly the same?
Although this sounds like a prank, it's actually
FACT! Did we fool you?

TOOTHY TALES

Do you know anyone with braces? A dental company had a brilliant idea: 'canine aligners' for straightening the teeth of DOGS! What a silly **FOOL!** Surely no one believed this one!

FURRY AND FASHIONABLE

A famous magazine called *National Geographic* once announced that they would no longer be publishing photos of naked animals, to preserve our furry friends' dignity. Ha ha! Definitely a **FOOL!** I mean, would **YOU** try and put pants on a grizzly bear?!

THE GREATEST PRANK OF ALL TIME

BEST PRANK EVER

THE ALIENS HAVE LANDED!

Aliens. Do they exist? Like, REALLY?! I've never met one, so I'm not convinced. But what if you HEARD them with your very own ears?

Do you know someone really, really old? If you do, they might remember a time before television. Sounds crazy, doesn't it? What did people even DO before telly?! (Apart from reading awesome books, like the one you're reading right now!) Well, instead of watching telly, people listened to the radio . . . which is what millions of Americans were doing the night the aliens landed.

Can you imagine? You turn the radio on and rather than normal radio stuff (snore), you hear shouting and screaming. A reporter on the scene tries to stay calm as he announces that an alien spacecraft has crash-landed. He describes clouds of black gas and then he starts to panic as he sees **ACTUAL, REAL-LIFE ALIENS** emerging! America is being invaded! **HELP!**

The next voice you hear is the president, telling you to stay calm . . . which means it's definitely time to panic. Now you know for sure that this is . . .

THE BIGGEST EMERGENCY THE WORLD HAS EVER SEEN!!!!

...OR IS IT?

While Americans panicked, a writer called Orson Welles was celebrating his mind-blowing prank. There were no aliens, only actors! It was just a radio play, based on a super scary alien story called *War of the Worlds*. But it was **SO GOOD** that listeners believed it (just as Orson had planned!).

So, would you have fallen for the greatest prank of all time? Why not give it a go yourself? Look out of the window and say, **'ARGH! Aliens!'** and see who you can fool!

what if aliens do exist and they are already here on earth but they are really small so you cant see them but they can see you and they live in your nose actually maybe thats why bogeys are green maybe bogeys are green aliens hmm

PRANKS FOR SPECIAL OCCASIONS

i think a funny christmas prank would be to tell your family on christmas day that the turkey is ready and then when they come into the dining room there is a real live turkey sitting at the table wearing a santa hat and holding a cracker ha ha but it would probably be hard to get a live turkey and also they dont speak your language so if you are saying to them DO YOU WANT MORE SPROUTS you wouldnt be able to work out if they DO or DONT

LOVE IS IN THE AIR

The whole point of a Valentine's card is that no one knows who it's from, right? So, have a little fun!

BE MY VALENTINE

Draw a lovely, smoochy card saying, 'YOU ARE MY VALENTINE! I LOVE YOU THE MOST IN THE WHOLE WORLD!' to your parent. Then sign it from your family pet. Woof!

I HE-AAARGH-T YOU!

Buy a self-recording card, but instead of a cutesy 'I love you' message, record yourself doing a **BLOOD-CURDLING SCREAM.**

Extra Prank Points: *let off a whoopee cushion or a fart machine sound every time someone says something soppy on Valentine's Day!*

CHOC SHOCK

Plan ahead for this one by keeping hold of discarded packaging. Fill an empty chocolate box with cabbage or something else a bit gross. Give it to your 'Valentine' then giggle as they open your very thoughtful gift . . .

FONT FUN

Ask an adult to help you sneak into your family computer and change the font to a really romantic one. Whoever uses it first that day will have surprise hearts all over their writing!

i can never get on the family computer because there is always someone else on it and theyre usually on Amazon buying something and then when it arrives theyre like why did i buy this ive got enough socks already

HALLOWEEN HOWLERS

Watch out! There is no better time for pranks than Halloween . . .

CREEPY CUT-OUTS

Did you read about the Cottingley Fairies on page 46? Now it's your turn! Use card to make cut-outs of a witch, ghost or creepy critter. In a dark room, position a lamp or torch so that it shines on your cut-outs and makes a spooky shadow appear on the wall. Now, here comes the fun bit . . . pretend that you are FREAKING OUT!

GHASTLY GHOSTS

Sneak outside, knock at the front door, then run away before your family opens it. There will be no one there! Must be a ghost, right?!

Extra Prank Points: use a stick to make scary scratching sounds at the windows! Argh! Monsters!

i went to a halloween party the drinks were served by skeleton staff ha ha ask a grown-up they will explain it to you

HAUNTED HOUSE

But, really, on Halloween, you want to go ALL OUT. Why not surprise your family with a fully staged haunted house in one room? Turn the page for some truly terrifying ideas . . .

Ask a grown-up to download a **creeaaaakkky** sound effect on their phone. Play it every time the door opens!

Put torches or small LED lights inside empty loo-roll tubes and put them in dark corners to look like eyes staring out of the dark.

Dress up as a vampire, ghost or zombie, and jump out at your family, shouting, **'BOO!'**

Ask an adult to help you balance a net containing fake spiders on top of the door. Leave the door ajar - when your family walks into the room, the fake web will fall, releasing the fake spiders!

Leave some 'severed limbs' lying around. You can make a brilliant severed arm or leg using papier mâché (see page 37 for instructions).

Even better, just come down for breakfast dressed as something terrifying. EVEN, EVEN better? Come down for breakfast dressed normally EXCEPT for one strange spooky element like . . .

fake blood dripping from your mouth like a vampire

Frankenstein bolts sticking out of your head

one side of your face coloured greenish-grey with face paints

. . . then act like nothing is wrong – while stopping yourself from laughing!

DEJA VU

Wrap up something the birthday boy or girl already owns and give it to them like it's brand new. (Give them an actual present too!)

ALL WRAPPED UP

Wrap up EVERYTHING – their toothbrush, their cereal bowl, their shoes . . .

CALENDAR CHAOS!

Get your whole family to pretend they forgot your sibling's birthday. Then surprise them with a party!

when my pet rabbit turned three last month i made her a card saying hoppy birthday ha ha i dont think she can actually read but i feel like she got it

EGGCELLENT EASTER

I love chocolate but I hate hunting for it. Like, just let me eat it already, Easter Bunny, hey? If your grown-up insists on making you work for your Easter chocolate, get your own back . . .

Use your super sleuth skills to find out where the chocolate stash is hidden BEFORE Easter, then . . .

replace the eggs with a note from the Easter Bunny saying, 'Too slow!'

replace the eggs with Christmas decorations. That'll confuse everyone!

hide the eggs yourself . . . in super super sneaky places!

CHRISTMAS CRACKERS

At Christmas, you can play present pranks on the WHOLE FAMILY – ho ho ho!

FESTIVE FRUSTRATION

When you're wrapping presents for your family, use extra tape to seal down every single edge of wrapping paper – making your family's gifts really, really impossible to open!

EXTREME UNBOXING

Wrap things in a series of boxes so it looks like a HUGE present but once you get to the last box, it's actually teeny tiny. Ha ha!

i love christmas so much you could say im christmas crackers ha ha do you get it

WHO . . . ?!

Write a label from a completely made-up relative and stick it on a present – your family will be so confused!

WHAT . . . ?!

Disguise a present so that it's a completely different shape. What is the silliest thing you could put under the tree or in someone's stocking?!

PUZZLE PRANK

Put crushed-up Weetabix in a see-through food bag, then make a label that says **'Expert-level Jigsaw Puzzle, One Million Pieces'**.

POO BAG

Bag up some marshmallows and make a label that says **'snowman poo'**.

No other days in the year to prank? Nope.
No, I really can't think of any. No . . .

APRIL FOOL!

YOU THOUGHT WE'D FORGOTTEN APRIL FOOL'S DAY! WE PRANKED YOU!

The 1 April is the most important day of the year for pranksters - bigger than Easter, bigger than Christmas. Even grown-ups get involved. So have fun, go wild . . . now is the time to dream up your **best prank ever!**

THE VERY FIRST FOOL

April Fool's Day began many, many, many, many, MANY years ago in Roman times. In his royal court, the Emperor Constantine had a jester (or 'fool') called Kugel. One day, Kugel told the emperor that HE could do a better job of running the empire than Constantine did. Ha ha! thought Constantine, I'd like to see that! So he let Kugel be king for a day.

Silly idea? No . . . AMAZING idea! Kugel told everyone to have fun and do silly pranks ALL DAY LONG! People loved it so much that they decided to have a day of silliness EVERY year. The date was – yes, you've guessed it – 1 April!

What a great tale, right? **Um, read on . . .**

It's totally made up! But not by me . . .
A very serious professor of History invented
the story and told it to a newspaper reporter
. . . who believed it. **CLANG! The ultimate
April Fool's fool!** The weird thing is, despite
it being fake news, a lot of people STILL believe
the story today!

So, what will **YOU** do this April Fool's Day?
One showstopping prank or a day filled with
mini pranks? Here are some super silly ideas
to get you started . . .

i would have
believed it but then
i believe anything to
be honest like i thought
jurassic park actually
happened

FOOL'S DAY FUN

FREAKY FRIDGE

Stick googly eyes on jars and cartons in the fridge, and even eggs! (Don't put googly eyes on anything that isn't wrapped.)

FOOD FACE-OFF

Draw faces on food! Use any pen for eggs or hard-peel fruit like oranges. For anything with edible skin, you'll need a food-colouring pen.

WIBBLE WOBBLE WHOA!

Serve a glass of juice that is really jelly with a straw in it! (Ask an adult to help you prepare the jelly the night before.)

EX-SQUEEZE ME?

Take a bottle with a cap, like a shampoo bottle, unscrew the cap and carefully cover the top with clingfilm or sellotape (ask an adult to help if you're using clingfilm). Replace the cap. Your family will not be able to work out why they can't get the shower gel out! Ha ha ha!

PEA IN THE EAR

Hide a cooked pea in your hand and pretend to find it in your ear. Now eat it. **GROSS!**

Extra Prank Points: *'find' a pea in someone else's ear!*

94

LOLLY LOLS

Cover a Brussels sprout in chocolate to look like a lollipop. A carrot on the end of a stick will work well too. Wait for the chocolate-covered veg to cool then put it back in the wrapper. Watch and giggle as someone unwraps a yucky veg lolly.

Ask an adult to help you make melted chocolate. Heat broken chocolate squares gently in a pan on the stove or zap a bowl of chocolate for ten seconds at a time in the microwave. (No one wants burnt chocolate - yuck!)

95

FERRERO ROCH-HEY!

Brussels sprouts ALSO fit into Ferrero Rocher wrappers . . . if you're interested . . . don't tell anyone I told you . . . NO, I'm not telling you to replace all the chocolates with Brussels sprouts. You'd have to be way too careful and neat and tidy. And then what would you do with all the chocolate you'd taken out? You'd have to eat it to hide the evidence.

Nightmare! Definitely don't do this one.

PRANKS THAT WENT WRONG

of course not all pranks go as planned so
this chapter features some disasters i once
done a prank that went wrong i put chilli
and Tabasco sauce in my brothers chicken
soup but then I got confused and
gave him the wrong bowl which
meant i ate it instead it
tasted of YUK

PEPPER
SAUCE

PULLING THE WOOL

Scientists prank reporters ... again!

Woolly mammoths lived in dinosaur times and they don't exist any more. They are EXTINCT. So when a team of Russian scientists, led by Dr Sverbighooze Nikhiphorovitch Yasmilov (**DING DING DING**, silly name alert!), said they were using super clever science to bring a woolly mammoth back to life, it was **OBVIOUSLY A PRANK!** But one American newspaper believed the story and published it. It was read by thousands of people ... who also believed it. The newspaper had to apologise for reporting fake news! Oh dear ... mammoth mistake!

TICK TOCK!

On their last day in high school, American teenagers often plan huge pranks. But sometimes they prank TOO HARD.

Two students from North Carolina thought it would be funny for alarm clocks to go off every few minutes all around school. So they put clocks in unused lockers, sat back and waited to giggle. But what else ticks? Yeah ... bombs. The school totally panicked, called the Army Bomb Squad and the two pranksters were **ARRESTED**. Be prank-smart. Think it through, people.

if anyone in your house still uses a clock radio then its kind of funny to turn it up so its really loud when they wake up but then actually thinking about it it will probably wake you up too so maybe dont

PRESIDENTIAL PRANK

An Icelandic teenager, Vífill Atlason, was bored one day and tried to call the president of the USA (who was George W. Bush at the time). He was so convincing pretending to be Ólafur Ragnar Grímsson, the actual Icelandic president, that he was put through to President Bush's direct line! He was told that the president would call him back the next day . . . but in fact the Icelandic police turned up and took him to the police station for questioning.

Pranks have definitely gone too far if you get arrested!

THE ULTIMATE CLIFFHANGER

In 2001,
a DJ decided
to prank his radio
audience that a ship
looking like the *Titanic*
had been spotted off the
cliffs of Beachy Head
in East Sussex.

But when **HUNDREDS** of listeners
flocked to the cliffs to take a look, they
caused a large **CRACK** in the cliff face.
The cliff then fell into the sea.

Happily no one was harmed.

MONSTER MESS

People have been looking for the mysterious Loch Ness Monster for centuries . . .

Legend says that a strange beast lurks in the deep waters of Loch Ness in Scotland. Lots of people claim to have seen 'Nessie' but no one has ever proved it. (Weird, that!)

So, when a team of animal scientists (called zoologists) discovered the body of a big, grey creature, they thought they had finally discovered the monster.

But . . . it was all a prank that got out of hand. 'Nessie' was actually a large bull elephant seal. A naughty prankster had shaved off its whiskers before putting it into the Loch.

DJ BUZZ-TED!

Watch out! The wasps are attacking!

'Mile-wide swarm of wasps heading towards town!'
That was the warning from radio DJ Phil Shone to
his listeners in Auckland, New Zealand, one April
Fool's Day back in 1949. 'Wear socks over your
trousers!' Phil told them. 'Leave traps smeared
with honey outside your front door!' (As if that
would help?!)

Well, the people of Auckland **PANICKED!** They
had no internet to check the facts ... just radio.

DJ Phil quickly admitted it was all a joke. But the
New Zealand Broadcasting Service did **NOT** find
it funny. Now, every year, they remind their radio
stations to report nothing but the truth ...
even on April Fool's Day!

GREAT MOON HOAX

Ever wondered what's on the Moon? No, because astronauts have actually been there and it's just boring rocks and stuff.

But before that, everyone thought the Moon was super mysterious and interesting and, hey, maybe aliens lived there or it was made of cheese ... who knew? People's imaginations went totally wild.

Then one day, in 1835, an American newspaper reported an incredible discovery. Using a powerful new telescope, scientists had looked at the Moon's surface for the first time and seen **WINGED BAT PEOPLE!** Yes, the Moon was inhabited by humans with wings like bats! Amazing! There were also rivers, plants, beavers, goats and ... unicorns!

Of course, it was a **HOAX!**

The thing is, the reporter who wrote the article wasn't trying to trick people. No one knew much about the Moon back then, and lots of people were making up weird 'facts' about it. (One fake story said that there were billions of humans living there!) The reporter wanted his joke to show people they shouldn't believe everything they were told. There was only one problem... readers thought it was **TRUE** and begged for **more detail!** D'oh!

if you dont have any astronauts then you have astronoughts ha ha

LAVA DRAMA

Once again, it was the pranksters who lost out when their horrifying hoax ERUPTED!

In 1980, a TV station in Boston, USA, reported that a nearby peak, Great Blue Hill, was spewing lava in a surprise **volcanic eruption!** They showed a dramatic video of molten lava pouring down the side of the hill. The date was 1 April and the hill was . . . just a hill. But local residents freaked out anyway! The producer who thought up the prank was sacked. Epic fail!

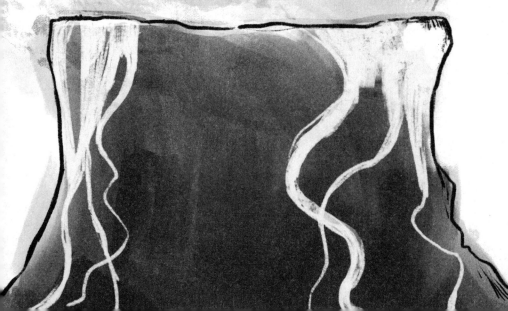

PRANKS TO PLAY ON HOLIDAY

one time i was on holiday in spain and i had an idea for a prank and i went into a shop and pretended i was spanish but it didnt really work because i dont speak spanish apart from 'no hablo español' which is spanish for 'i dont speak spanish' thats all i know and the lady who worked in the shop was spanish and she realised straight away and i got all embarrassed and didnt know what to do and i panicked and bought a pencil sharpener which i didnt even need anyway the good news is that the pranks in this chapter are better than that one which isnt hard

107

MATT'S MARVELLOUS

Roll up, roll up, get your classic pranks here! All the pranks you'll ever need! What will you buy . . . ?

Whoopee cushion

Plastic beetles/flies/ cockroaches - put them anywhere, e.g. drawers, school lunch box

Fake blood

FFFFTT!

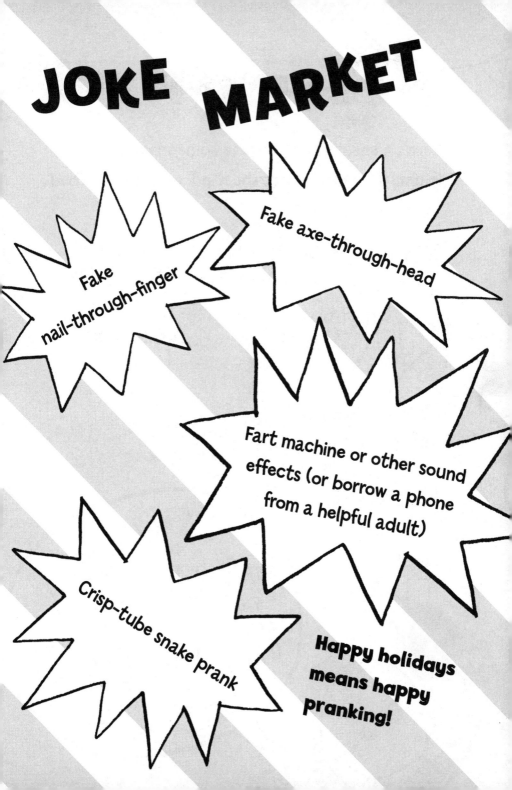

APPLE PIE BED

Here's a sneaky trick to give someone a night fright. It's called 'short sheeting' or 'apple pie bed'.

1.

Untuck the sheet from the end of the bed. Pull the corners up till they're level with the pillow, then tuck them under the mattress. The sheet should be folded now – like a sleeping bag made of sheet!

2.

When your sibling gets into bed – well – they won't be able to! Their feet will only fit halfway down. Ha ha!

holidays are great
if you want to spend
all your savings and fly
halfway across the world and sit
by a crowded pool and get stuck
talking to some people who it
turns out live in the street
next to yours

MIRROR MIRROR ON THE WALL

With only paper, a pen and some sticky tape, you can cause chaos on holiday . . .

Tape this sign up on your holiday mirror (be sure to disguise your handwriting):

MIRROR UNDER REPAIR.

PLEASE DO NOT USE.

WONKY WARDROBE

Sometimes it's hard to prank without props. Not these pranks. All you need is clothes.

Dress with all your clothes on backwards. Pretend like nothing's wrong. This is especially funny if you use a hat to hide your face. Stand and wait for someone to say hello to what they think is your back, then wave your arms in front of you - as if they are coming out of your back!

Dress up in your dad's board shorts, T-shirt and flip-flops. The smaller you are compared to him, the better. Pretend like nothing's wrong.

Go to the beach wearing your coat and a winter woolly hat. Pretend like nothing's wrong.

LIFT LOLS

If you're **SUPER** sneaky, you could put up a sign in the hotel lift saying 'Floor 3 is missing'. Maybe even put a sign up over the third floor sign itself saying 'This floor does not exist'. Fool your fellow holiday guests – they'll be so confused!

BROLLY LOLS

When someone's lying on a sun lounger, keep carefully moving the umbrella so they are in the shade all day. They'll think it's so strange that the sun is moving and their shade is not!

BURIED TREASURE

Bury a small chest of chocolate gold coins. Dig them back up and shout, **'Arrr, me hearties! Treasure!'** You could also bury fake dinosaur bones and create a surprise dig on the beach. (Don't forget to dig up everything you bury.)

PRANK CHALLENGE
BINGO

Copy the grid and fill in the squares when you've done a prank involving each of the items. First one to a full house wins!

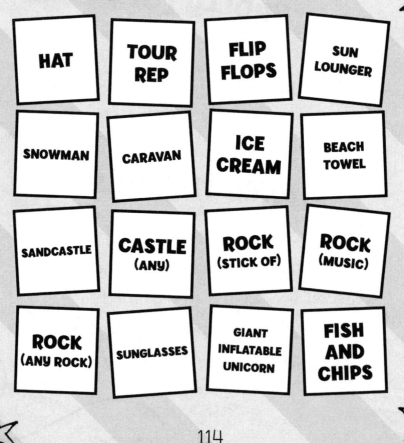

HAT	TOUR REP	FLIP FLOPS	SUN LOUNGER
SNOWMAN	CARAVAN	ICE CREAM	BEACH TOWEL
SANDCASTLE	CASTLE (ANY)	ROCK (STICK OF)	ROCK (MUSIC)
ROCK (ANY ROCK)	SUNGLASSES	GIANT INFLATABLE UNICORN	FISH AND CHIPS

ROCK BOTTOM

Fool someone with just a simple rock plus
a pen or Post-it note . . .

Step 1: find a rock.

Step 2: on the front of the rock write 'TURN ME OVER'.

Step 3: on the bottom of the rock write 'You just took orders from a rock'.

Step 4: leave the rock somewhere and wait for someone to find it.

Step 5: LAUGH OUT LOUD!

Other funny things you could write:

IN CASE OF FIRE
TURN ME OVER.

NOT NOW, SILLY!
IN CASE OF FIRE!

TURN ME OVER TO
FIND OUT WHAT
YOU'VE WON.

ABSOLUTELY
NOTHING!

TURN ME
OVER

NOPE. I'VE
CHANGED MY
MIND

sorry this page went on holiday

HEE HE HEEE !

PRANKSTERS' HALL OF FAME

DAWN JUNE RUSSELL ANGELA

if you didnt know a hall of fame is a list
of the best people in that particular field
which if it was a farmers hall of fame
would probably be one with some cows in

Name: Ant and Dec
Famous for: being Ant and Dec, presenting top telly together
Best prank: Fake Audition

So, you know Ant and Dec presented *Britain's Got Talent* with Simon Cowell ... who was also a judge on *American Idol?* One day, Ant and Dec snuck into the *American Idol* auditions in order to prank him. Dressed up as two brothers, they did a TERRIBLE audition. Simon got more and more annoyed as the two brothers refused to leave the room. Finally Ant and Dec pulled off their disguises - they'd tricked the trickiest man on telly!

i love ant and dec but when they are in the jungle i always wonder if they will be eaten by a tiger in the middle of the show i hope not

Simon forgave Ant and Dec, then the three of them pranked Piers Morgan by *pretending* to break a priceless piece of art! Oops!

Prank rating: 8/10 - Ant and Dec get really famous people to look really, REALLY silly.

Try this at home rating: 7/10 - you can definitely prank your school drama teacher by doing a fake terrible audition for the school play. But don't tell your dad you broke his favourite vase - he might be furious!

Name: Lucas Mathews

Famous for: being the greatest prankster of all time.

Top pranks: how to choose . . . ?!

Mathews is the world's best AND most mysterious prankster. No one knows what he looks like, although we believe he wears a suit made of peas. No one knows how old he is either, because, like a koala, he has a different number of birthdays every year.

Mathews' birthday pranks are world-famous. Once he turned the sea between the UK and France to jelly and invited everyone in the two countries to come and bounce on it. There were so many people bouncing that the jelly exploded and all of Europe got splattered. Another time, he lit so many candles on his enormous birthday cake that the Moon began to melt.

i wish I could have met him he sounds so funny

In another famous prank, Mathews picked his nose on live TV and pulled out a kangaroo. No one has ever found out how he did it, but he and the kangaroo have been best friends ever since!

Prank rating: 10/10 - spectacular pranks that make the whole world gasp (in alarm).
Try this at home rating: 1/10 - leave nose-picking to the professionals - you don't know what you might find up there!

Name: Jeremy Beadle
Famous for: *Beadle's About*
Best prank ever: Alien Arrival

TV prankster Jeremy Beadle was not afraid to GO BIG. His best prank was turning a woman's back garden into an **ALIEN LANDING SITE** with a huge crater. When the woman got home, she was met by local police and reporters, who were in on the prank. She totally believed it! Well, wouldn't you? And when the alien emerged ... she offered it a cup of tea!

Prank rating: 11/10 super gold stars
Try this at home rating: 6/10 - Jeremy went **ALL OUT**. Be inspired and create an elaborate prank that your family will remember for years!

Name: Adele

Famous for: being a superstar singer

Best prank ever: pretending to be herself

Singer Adele came up with the perfect prank when she entered a competition for Adele impersonators! She called herself Jenny, wore a fake nose and chin, and spoke in a different voice. She even pretended to have stage fright! The other 'Adeles' were totally fooled. But as she started to sing, one of the 'Adeles' spotted the prank, and soon everyone was laughing, crying . . . and singing along!

Prank rating: 10/10 – a pitch-perfect prank with lots of preparation!

Try this at home rating: 7/10 – why not swap places with a friend or sibling for the day. Say what they'd say, do what they'd do . . .

Name: Allen Funt

Famous for: *Candid Camera* – the ORIGINAL TV prank show, 1960s

Best prank ever: The Car With No Engine

When Allen Funt found a car without an engine in a local scrapyard, he had an idea. He got an actress to pretend to be the driver then secretly pushed the car into a garage. The driver got out to asked the mechanic for help. The mechanic lifted the bonnet and saw . . . no engine! HOW did a car without an engine drive into his garage?!?!

Prank rating: 10/10 - elaborate, tons of effort. Bravo, Alan, bravo!

you will never fool me with this one because i dont have a car because i cant drive because i failed my driving test seven times so whos the idiot now ha ha oh

Try this at home rating: 3/10 - it's not a great idea to take an engine out of a car at home. I mean, where would you put it? But you **COULD** make fake parking tickets for your little brother or sister's toy cars and send them to get towed away!

Other great *Candid Camera* pranks:

 giving an out-of-control tennis ball machine to a group of kids to practise on

 rigging windscreen wipers on a car to squirt passers-by

 altering supermarket trollies so that shoppers could only turn them in circles!

Name: Dom Joly
Famous for: *Trigger Happy TV*
Best pranks: Fancy dress fun!

What's the funniest thing you've ever seen
on a zebra crossing? TV prankster Dom Joly
disguised himself as a human-sized SNAIL,
crossing the road veerrry veerrry slooowwllyy.
He also called a rat-catcher to his house and
answered the door dressed as a giant RAT! Ha!

Prank rating: 9/10 - all hail the KING of
DISGUISE!
Try this at home rating: 10/10 -

use fancy dress to
create some wild
pranks!

this is one of my
favourite tv shows as well
as Pingu but my worst show is
the news it is soooooooooooooooooooo
boring all these things happened so
what who cares just show us
a cartoon

Name: Justin Bieber
Famous for: being the Prince of Pop
Top prank: Payback Prank

Most celebs hate gossip magazines. No one likes being talked about behind their back! One April Fool's Day, popstar Justin Bieber got his own back. He tweeted his fans to tell them he was going to answer ALL their calls. He posted a number and the phone started ringing . . . but it wasn't his own phone! It was the number for a gossip magazine, which was swamped with annoying calls! Ouch!

Prank rating: 9/10 – Justin's fans found the prank hilarious . . . once they'd got over their disappointment!
Try this at home rating: 0/10 – definitely don't try this at home.

Names: *Rank the Prank,*
Just Kidding, Little Pranksters
Famous for: brilliant hidden camera shows ...
starring KIDS!
Top pranks: *sooooo* many amazing pranks

There is **NOTHING** funnier than watching grown-ups
getting pranked by kids! These expert TV pranksters
trick adults into believing they can lift enormous
buckets of coins, swallow swords, make plates of
spaghetti explode ... and even disappear and
magically reappear somewhere else (it was actually
identical twins!).

Prank rating: 10/10 - epic pranks
that make grown-ups' heads spin!
Try this at home rating: 6/10 -
these elaborate pranks are best left to
the professionals! Sit back and enjoy!

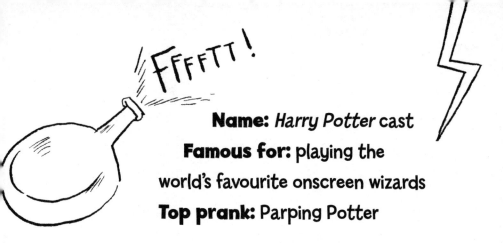

Name: *Harry Potter* cast
Famous for: playing the world's favourite onscreen wizards
Top prank: Parping Potter

It isn't just kids who find farts funny. The actors playing Severus Snape and Dumbledore in the *Harry Potter* movies once put a fart machine inside Daniel Radcliffe (Harry Potter)'s sleeping bag before filming a scene. Hearing Harry Potter let out a massive PARP made everyone giggle. Harry, you're one windy wizard!

Prank rating: 9/10 – it's a classic!
Try this at home rating: 10/10 – give this prank a magical twist! Make yourself a magic wand then wave it just before your victim sits on your carefully hidden whoopee cushion! Expelliarmus!

Name: The Queen

Famous for: being the Queen. Also, in private, being a top prankster! (Apparently she's very good at mimicking people's accents.)

Silliest prank: Philip's Face!

In 1956, Prince Philip, the Queen's husband, went on a six-month tour of Australia and Antarctica all by himself (well, on a boat with loads of Navy sailors). While away, he grew a beard for the first time. For his welcome home party, the Queen arranged for everyone to wear fake beards. Ha ha, good one, Your Majesty!

Prank rating: 10/10 - she's the Queen, bow down!

Try this at home rating: 9/10 - you could totally copy this royal prank!

GUESS WHAT - we pranked you! Did you spot that one of the talented pranksters in this chapter is **totally made up?**

Haven't spotted who it is yet? Look at the names for a clue!

Who or what can **YOU** convince your friends and family to believe in? A new teacher? A new pet?!

YOUR PRANKS

these pranks were sent in by readers so if you dont like them dont blame me and if you do like them then i take all the credit for so generously letting other people contribute to my book i should have charged them a fee really

MAIL BAG

Once on April Fool's Day, my mum and dad said that some man-eating plants had come into our house and were downstairs. I was very scared because I was only 4.

Tim, aged 7

When my mum makes meringues she puts them in a box called Cabbage so my dad won't eat them.

Tyler, age 7

I did a poo in my brother's bed. Hahaha not really!

Ruby, age 6

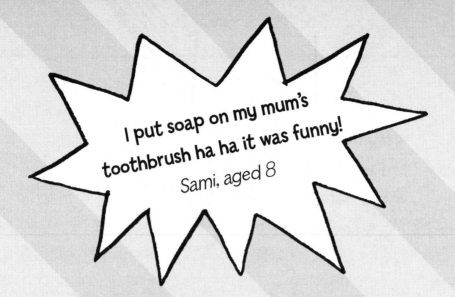

I put soap on my mum's toothbrush ha ha it was funny!

Sami, aged 8

I had a boiled egg for tea and I turned the empty egg shell upside down and put it in the egg cup. I gave it to my sister and she thought it had egg inside. I laughed a lot.

Jake, age 9

On April Fool's Day, we pretended that the our chickens had escaped and gone into our neighbour's garden! My mum and dad were in a panic, and they were cross when they found out it was a prank.

Rebecca, aged 8

My friend and I dressed up as ghosts
to scare our friends on a sleepover but
we were so scared of actual ghosts
that we didn't do it!

Eli, age 9

When I stayed at my aunt and uncle's,
my uncle put a fake bat in my bed.
I will get him back!

Zara, age 7

I did a prank with my dad. We put
a pillow on top of the door then when
my mum opened it, it fell on her head.

Vivi, age 11

136

My brother and I hid all the Christmas presents from under the tree and we put empty boxes and ripped-up wrapping paper there instead. When my parents came down in the morning, it looked like we'd opened all the presents!

Harriet, aged 10

On Christmas Eve, I woke my sister up and shouted, 'Wake up, it's Christmas!' She ran downstairs to see what Santa had left her and then I said it wasn't actually Christmas yet! My parents said I was naughty and Santa might not give me any presents!

Melissa, age 8

We can't wait any longer.

Get ready . . .
here they come . . .

VERY VERY VERY VERY VERY VERY VERY YUCKY PRANKS

who doesnt love a YUCKY prank like leaving a fake poo in the bath ha ha and if you say you dont you are lying lets face it we are all human we all have yucky things coming out of us sometimes and lets be honest youre probably reading this on the toilet anyway dont forget to flush

POO PRANKS

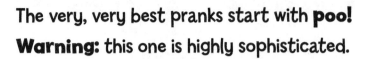

The very, very best pranks start with **poo!**
Warning: this one is highly sophisticated.

Now, you can get fake poos from joke shops, but
you can also bake biccies that look like poop
(recipe opposite). Here comes the clever and
sophisticated part . . . **LEAVE THE FAKE POO IN
FUNNY PLACES! ANYWHERE YOU LIKE!**

ha ha fooled you its
not clever or sophisticated
at all

Leave poos all over the house. Somewhere like
actually on the loo seat would be extra funny!
If you have a pet, blame the poos on them!

Extra Prank Points: PRETEND TO EAT THE
PRETEND POO!!! **EWWW!!!** (Not the one
that's been on the loo seat obviously!)

please make sure you have read this properly because nobody will be very happy if you make a biscuit out of a actual poo though im not gonna lie some of the food in the school canteen is probably worse ha ha

To make chocolate poo biccies you will need:

100g butter, softened

50g caster sugar

125g self-raising flour

15g cocoa powder

1 helpful grown-up

Ask your grown-up to preheat the oven to 180°C / 350°F. Line a baking tray with baking paper. Mix the butter and sugar together in a large bowl till soft. Mix in the flour and cocoa. Roll the dough into 12 poo-shaped biscuits and place on the baking sheet. Bake for 12-15 minutes then leave to cool on a wire rack. **Ta-da! Chocolate poo!**

143

NASTY NAPPIES

Got a baby in your house? Here's a really gross trick . . .

Get a clean nappy, smear chocolate spread on it and leave it lying around for your family to find. If you really want to freak everyone out, try sniffing it, then . . . licking it! **Ewwwww!**

Did you know that baby poos can be **REALLY, REALLY WEIRD?** There are LOADS of things around the house look like super icky types of baby poo. Why not try:

- **Green food colouring**
- **Raisins**
- **Peanut butter** (smooth AND crunchy)
- **Chocolate milkshake**

Now, keep your fake baby fake pooping!

What's almost as gross as poo? Snot, of course!

SNOTTY SURPRISE

Politely tell a friend or family member that they have a snotty nose. They'll probably be embarrassed . . . especially when they wipe their nose and you tell them it's still there!

BOGUS BOGIES

Prepare a tissue with something gross on it, like a blob of porridge with a drop of green food dye in it. Pretend to wipe your nose, then examine the tissue. Eww! Show it around and gross everyone out with your totally bogus bogies!

Extra Prank Points: *is your fake bogey make of something edible? If so . . . eat it!*

i am a great actor i even been in films and i was so good in them i am now writing books for kids

If you can get your mitts on some dried fruit, there is no end to the fun you can have. This prank requires a bit of ACTING, DARLING . . .

SILLY FLY SWATTING

Pretend you can see a fly buzzing around. Act like it's really annoying you. Try to catch it and fail a couple of times. SECRETLY you've had a small raisin hiding in your hand the whole time. Now 'catch' the fly. Smack! Gotcha! Hold it out to show someone, then . . . eat the 'fly'! **EWWWW!!**

Extra Prank Points: borrow a phone from a helpful friend or grown-up and play the sound of a fly buzzing. Sit back as everyone runs around trying to find it!

Shhhh! Here's another messy one . . .

STICK 'EM UP

This is just between you and me, right? Replace hand soap with honey or syrup. When someone tries to pump it out to wash their hands, they'll get stickier and stickier!

honey is harder to come by these days because the bees went on strike over shorter working flowers ha ha

CREEPY CRITTERS

Leave currants out in the corners of your kitchen. 'Discover' them, eat one, grimace and say, 'Yup, definitely mouse droppings.' Now watch as your parents try to decide what to panic about first: mice in the house or you eating mouse poo! **SERIOUSLY EURGH!!!**

FINGER IN THE BOX

Cut out the bottom of a matchbox and secretly poke your finger through the hole. Ask someone to look inside, revealing your 'severed' finger – **argh!**

Extra Prank Points: *put your finger on a bed of cotton wool and use ketchup to make it look **super gross** and awful.*

Super Duper Extra Prank Points:

with a bigger box, and a friend, replace the finger with an entire leg or arm or even your head.

talking of fingers have you ever seen a fish with fingers no me neither i reckon fish fingers are a CON they are nice though

LOO ROLL LOLS

All you need for this prank is a felt-tip pen.
And some loo roll, of course.

Unroll several sheets, being careful not to tear
them from the roll. Then write a message or
draw a picture. Go wild!

Draw a spider, making it as realistic as you can!

Write 'Help, I'm stuck in a toilet-paper factory!'

Draw your family members sitting on the loo!

Now wind the paper back around and wait for
someone to get a super silly surprise!

i know its very important to think about the environment but i draw the line at second-hand toilet paper

BOW TO THE BOWL

Some people call the toilet 'a throne'. So why not dress it up like a throne? Make a fancy crown. Give it a cloak (old curtains are always good). Make up a name for your new toilet ruler and a list of rules for its loyal subjects!

LOO ROLL SWAP

Take the toilet roll off the toilet roll holder and replace it with something else on a roll, like Sellotape. Very simple . . . super annoying!

Extra Prank Points: *close the toilet lid then arrange two loo rolls on top to look like eyes.* **Ta-da** *- toilet frog!*

WHOOPEE WHOOPEE EVERYWHERE!

Here are some ideas for having fun with everyone's favourite prank prop, the whoopee cushion!

FANCY COFFEE SHOP - you know those cafés with lots of mums and babies? Let off your whoopee cushion and blame it on a baby.

BOTTY BURP BUS RIDE - bored on the bus? Let your bottom blasts blare!

LOO QUEUE - you may not be the only one who's struggling to keep it in.

WHAT'S FOR DINNER? - a classic, especially when cabbage or sprouts are on the menu.

TOWN CLOCK - park your behind on the cushion just as the clock on the town hall or church tower strikes the hour. Say, 'Right on time.'

see page 44 for instructions

PARIS
IN THE
THE SPRING

Matt Lucas

MATT LUCAS is an actor, writer, comedian and very silly person. He became famous by playing a big baby who played the drums in a crazy TV show called *Shooting Stars*. His next TV show after that was called *Little Britain*, which he did with David Walliams. *Little Britain* was very rude indeed and you are not allowed to watch it until you are at least 75 years old.

Matt has played lots of other characters on TV, including Mr Toad in *The Wind in the Willows*, Bottom in *A Midsummer Night's Dream* (ha ha, I just said bottom) and the companion Nardole in *Doctor Who*, although it was too scary for Matt to watch. He has also appeared in

156

some Hollywood films, such as *Paddington*, and *Alice in Wonderland*, where he played Tweedle Dee and his equally silly brother, Tweedle Dum. Matt has also done voices for several cartoons, including Benny in *Gnomeo and Juliet*. Recently Matt has been presenting on *The Great British Bake Off* and also writing and singing about his friend, Baked Potato.

Matt loves to play pranks. A long time ago, before he was on TV, Matt worked in a shop and used to play a prank on the shopkeeper opposite. Every time the shopkeeper sat down to read his paper, Matt rang the shop. The shopkeeper had to get up to answer the phone. Matt hung up but as soon as the shopkeeper sat down, he did it again. The shopkeeper never knew Matt was in the shop opposite otherwise he would probably have told him off for being silly!

Sarah Horne

SARAH HORNE is an illustrator and writer. She first learned to draw aged nine, when she needed to explain to the hairdresser how she wanted her hair to be cut. The result was not what she had hoped for – but her picture was pretty amazing, even if she says so herself.

Since aged nine, Sarah's drawing has got better and better (and so have her haircuts). She has illustrated over 70 books, including *Charlie Changes into a Chicken* and *Fizzlebert Stump: The Boy Who Ran Away From the Circus (and Joined the Library)*, *Puppy Academy*, and *Ask Oscar* and its sequels. Most of the books she has drawn have been very, very silly.

Sarah didn't do many pranks as a kid – but when she DID, she was very convincing.
She once told a friend that she had spotted a cow without a head on the farm where her friend lived. Her friend believed her! The story spread and for weeks all their friends were looking for a headless cow roaming the fields.
Sarah found it very a-moo-sing!